MURDER
BY
MEMORY

MURDER BY MEMORY

BY

MEMORY

OLIVIA WAITE

T O R
D O T
C O M

Tor Publishing Group
New York

MURDER BY MEMORY

A Tordotcom Book
Published by Tom Doherty Associates / Tor Publishing Group
120 Broadway
New York, NY 10271

www.torpublishinggroup.com

Tor® is a registered trademark of Macmillan Publishing Group, LLC.

The Library of Congress Cataloging-in-Publication Data is available upon request.

ISBN 978-1-250-34224-9 (hardcover)
ISBN 978-1-250-34225-6 (ebook)

Our books may be purchased in bulk for promotional, educational, or business use. Please contact your local bookseller or the Macmillan Corporate and Premium Sales Department at 1-800-221-7945, extension 5442, or by email at MacmillanSpecialMarkets@macmillan.com.

First Edition: 2025

Printed in the United States of America

0 9 8 7 6 5 4 3 2 1

TO SARA AND IAN,
FOR THOSE LONG-AGO
SCI-FI TELEVISION REWATCHES.

AND TO CHARLES,
FOR THE STARGAZING.

MURDER
BY
MEMORY

NEAR THE TOPMOST DECK, IN A SMALL LIFT with glass walls and flickering buttons, I, Dorothy Gentleman, ship's detective, opened a pair of eyes and licked a pair of lips and awoke in a body that wasn't mine.

It was the nails that first tipped me off. Blank bodies were just that: blank. My nails ought to have been the same color as the skin beneath—in my case, somewhere in a range of pinks, tending to florid.

Not silver, and not shaped.

This body was already inhabited.

My skin—someone's skin—broke out in gooseflesh. Of course every human body was a horrifying collection of juices and tissues, acids and effluvia poured into a bag with a bunch of long rocks, a shambling accident of biology that made its own mysterious and often frustrating decisions without reference to the mind. They were disgusting miracles, every one.

It was always a bit unsettling to wake up in a fresh form, until habit made a home of it.

But someone else's home, and my self inside it! A nightmare. Imagine going to the washroom to be sick and having someone else's sick come out.

I came very close to making this more than a metaphor. It took many deep, deliberate breaths for the squeamish feeling to subside.

It wasn't supposed to be like this.

Normally one woke up in Medical, surrounded by institutional teal paint and staff with the kind of professionally soothing voices that made you want to claw your own skin off. Not in the central lift, which went only from the topmost three decks to the Library at the very peak of the ship.

Oh, the Library was a marvel. I wish you could have seen it.

Everyone on the *Fairweather* had a book and a body: the Library held a copy of your mind in the one while you walked around in the other. You could update your book as often as you pleased, adding in experiences and memories from your waking self. And when your body was damaged—in an accident, or from the inescapable progression of aging and illness—you could have your book-mind decanted into a new one based on your personal genetic pattern and preferences for sex. Et voilà, a whole new lifetime.

And if, say, you'd had a rather rough time of things

in your last body, you could rest for a time on the Library shelves, until you felt like being a human grappling with the world again.

I'd meant to be resting. I'd insisted, the last time I was asked. Yet here I was, contrary to my will, walking around on someone else's legs and running my thoughts with someone else's brain.

Something untoward must have happened.

"Ferry?" I queried, reaching out for the shipmind.

No response.

Not terribly odd: the *Fairweather*—Ferry for short—had a million different things to monitor at any one time. Unless it was actively listening, you sometimes had to wait a minute for your query to make it to the head of the queue. The lift had stopped—had been stopped?—between decks, and until I knew more about what was happening it seemed foolish to go blundering around like a bear escaped from a zoo.

To pass the time, I started riffling through my pockets.

Apparently the person who owned this body was fastidious: they'd chosen a fine white cotton shirt and gray wool suiting of elegant simplicity. My trouser and waistcoat pockets held only four things: an access card, a pocket watch in a sleek silvered case, a powder compact with a mirror, and a small electric torch engraved with ALL MY LOVE, V.

The pocket watch opened to reveal the usual bright

round screen. I held my thumb to it until it unlocked, then scrolled to the registration entry: Gloria Vowell, single, current body age twenty-seven. A clerk for one of the bank branches high on Forward Starboard Deck Three.

I had just about convinced myself that it was perfectly ethical to go digging for more information when Ferry deigned to respond.

Dorothy! the ship caroled, with a drunkard's delirious joy. But how could a shipmind be drunk? *I'm jolly glad you're awake! Had to put you in a what's a thing. Smallshape. Notship. Body!*

"So I gathered," I muttered. "But why?"

To save you! the ship went on. A giggle of triumph followed. *You're my favorite detective but don't tell anyone and I didn't want to lose you and now you're saved and everything is fiiiiiiiiiine!*

Everything was evidently not fine. I hadn't even been aware Ferry could impose a mind on a body not built for it. Perhaps that was a new development?

Perhaps everything was different?

I needed to get my bearings, and fast. "Ferry, what year is it?"

F307, came the swift reply. *F* for *Fairweather,* now more than three centuries into the millennium-long transit toward Whatever-We'll-Call-It. The number *307* made it two years since my last body had worn out in 305 and I'd had myself shelved. A lot could happen in two years, certainly, but probably not a complete breakdown of civil society.

Probably.

I pressed my face almost up against the glass, but it was night and the lights were dim and scattered, no people anywhere that I could see. "Ferry, what were you saving me from?"

Your memory-book got erased!

All the blood in my veins turned to ice, and I sat down, feeling faint.

But if my book was gone, then how was I here?

The ship was chattering on. *I was just trying to navigate and then all the alarms went wooga-wooga. To say a book was damaged. And when a ship's detective gets erased, my script says to put their secondary backup into the nearest body at once. But nobody in Medical. Or anyone on the bridge. Or Librarians. And there's a magnetic storm, so everyone else is battened down on the habitat decks—but Miss Vowell was right there in the lift. So you see I had to—what's a thing—impose.*

I squeezed my eyes shut, suspicion rising up thick and searing as heartburn. No need to ask who'd written that script and authorized the secondary backup that even I hadn't known about.

Whenever anything went frighteningly wrong in my life, one person was always at the root of it.

Rutherford Talmadge IV. The only son of my late sister, and one of Ferry's scriptwriters.

Oh, Ruthie was well-intentioned, even a genius in some very specific ways, but the boy had a talent for chaos that was an equal to the strong nuclear force. You could blindfold him, gag him, tie his hands, shackle his legs, put him in a room alone for five minutes—and when you returned Ruthie would still have found a way to lose all his money on a comet race or buy himself six shirts in a print so blindingly garish that lighthouses could use it in place of a beacon.

Ruthie was the reason I was on the *Fairweather* in the first place—and now it seemed he was the reason I had possessed someone, like a spirit summoned by an accidentally competent medium.

And like I said, Ruthie invariably meant well: if he'd done something this outrageous, it was to solve a problem. "Ferry, has anything else been damaged? Can you do a full self-inventory?"

A long, worrying pause—then the shipmind said in thoughtful tones: *You know, Dorothy, now that you mention it . . . I think somebody may be dead.*

The chill of my cold hands was a balm against throbbing temples. The shipmind was odd as a seven-winged duck, and didn't always appreciate the human point of view. "*May* be dead? Can you not say for certain either way?"

Good idea. Let's check.

I breathed in and out and tried to get a handle on my runaway exasperation. My nephew had authored so many of the ship's internal scripts over the centuries—no wonder certain commonalities of phrasing and expression crept in. Ferry babbling, the sense of tipsiness . . . This was easily the nephewest the shipmind had ever sounded. It boded not well.

Yes, said the ship, with what sounded suspiciously like a hiccup. I resisted the urge to speculate what a shipmind could even hiccup with. *There is definitely a new dead body in one of the passenger cabins. Aft Port Deck Sixteen, Janet Dodds. No vitals at all. I remember now I felt them die, but it was just as the magnetic storm started! So I couldn't send Medical—and then things got rather scrambly, and now they're just* there, *a blank spot interrupting all my comfortable scans.* The ship made a noise of profound unhappiness. *It itches.*

The magnetic storm—the only one I remembered—had happened two years ago. "Ferry, how many magnetic storms have there been since I got shelved?"

Thirteen.

I winced.

The science people say they're . . . something. About this corner of space. The quasars? So there may be many more of them.

The ship's mental voice was full of dread, and no wonder. Ruthie had once tried to explain—before I begged him to stop—how the first storm distorted the magnetics used in maintaining orientation and attitude. Redundancies kept the ship from abrupt physical changes in direction—say, turning the wrong way around and flinging us tiny humans up against the ceiling—but did not prevent the effects on the ship's sensors. Essentially, a magnetic storm turned Ferry into the ship equivalent of a bachelor on a bender.

This one's supposed to last until half ten, Ruthie told me. But the storms never killed anyone! They haven't even damaged anyone in the Library! A slight cough with metallic echoes. *Not since the first one, anyway.*

I shied away from that particular reminder. It was barely three months ago, for me. I wondered how Celia had spent the years since then . . .

My hands—I might as well start thinking of them as mine, since nobody else was using them—itched to get around a pair of knitting needles. Better to count stitches and rows and cable crosses than to dwell on what I'd lost. Or rather, what I'd kept, and what Celia had lost.

Ferry had begun to sing softly—something maudlin about sailors and rum and home.

The later stages of intoxication: I suspected I'd get nothing useful from this point forward. I asked for the address of the corpse, then gave strict instructions to do the shipmind version of sleeping it off.

The lift rang with the silence, now that it was just me and my own thoughts. Down the long decks below no doors were open, no passengers prowled the artificial night. Battened down, Ferry had said, and I was briefly grateful to be the only person awake. It gave me an opportunity.

A detective's book erased, and a fresh corpse killed at almost the same moment. I was willing to bet the timing was more than mere coincidence.

And one lone person out and about, who thanks to Ferry's imposition I couldn't even question.

Had Miss Vowell seen something? Was she a witness or an instigator? I'd have to wait to ask her, because for now I needed her body. It would be two long days before I could get a new one of my own—better to strike while the iron was hot, and before the trail had gone cold. We could always restore Miss Vowell's mind later, after all.

I pressed the button for Deck Sixteen and felt my stomach lurch as the descent began.

FROM LAUNCH, THE *FAIRWEATHER'S* COMMUnity Charter had been very clear that police were considered largely unnecessary. We had a small security force Ferry could deploy as needed—glorified bouncers, really—and a wealth of social workers in various fields; these two groups managed most everyday crises that arose.

For more complex situations—your elaborate hoaxes, your sudden deaths, your inexplicable accidents and incidents in which witness statements vastly differed—there were the ship's detectives. We had no power to arrest or enforce: our duty was strictly to sort out the truth from the lies and report them to the Crime Committee, which would arrange for any necessary punishments or reparations. I had volunteered as a lark in the first six months of the journey, and had surprised myself, at the age of fifty-seven, by finding my calling.

That was several lifetimes ago, and it had yet to turn tedious. Frustrating and disillusioning, sometimes, but never dull.

A detective's primary privilege was access, so when I reached the dead woman's apartment on Aft Port Deck Sixteen I reached out and offered my fingerprint to the lock. The doors slid open, and I stepped across the threshold.

Down here on Aft Port Sixteen the flats were sprawling, single-level affairs: a kitchen at the back, a bedroom and bathroom off the center hallway, and one large front room for entertaining company and/or any side business the occupant was involved in.

Miss Dodds's front room looked as though a wardrobe had exploded: garments in various states of construction and fabric samples were everywhere. Several sizes and genders of dress mannequins lurked headlessly in one corner. Colored pencil sketches on thin paper fluttered from the widest wall: skirts and trousers and evening wear, front and back pictured side by side. The retromat had recently produced a vivid silk print of clouds and cranes, folded in half and ready to be cut on the ruler-edged table shoved up close beneath the porthole on the farthest wall.

There were ever only the dark, distant stars outside instead of the warming sunlight or soothing rain of Old Earth, but somehow every human on board always put their worktables beneath their windows all the same. Myself included. As if we were careful to leave space in our lives for the weather we never experienced on board ship.

I moved closer to the wall of sketches. The same name was inked carefully in tiny capitals in the corner of every page: EMPYREAN DESIGNS.

The retromats, which fabricated objects from the operator's memories, were notoriously bad at producing clothing—at least, if you valued your dignity and were certain you wouldn't forget an important stitch or seam or zipper. But most people could make fabrics easily, and more than a few passengers on the *Fairweather* made extra money by creating and selling patterns to turn those fabrics into garments. Judging by the quantity and quality of designs I was seeing, Miss Dodds was more than a mere hobbyist.

I was halfway across the front room and headed for the rest of the apartment when the realization hit me: Dorothy Gentleman's body had a detective's privileges—but Gloria Vowell's didn't.

Which meant: the lock had recognized me. Gloria and the dead woman were connected.

It made sense, and I berated myself for not having thought of it earlier. Ferry had said everyone battened down during the storms—but there was Gloria, in the Library elevator, where she had no obvious business being.

I stopped where I was and pulled out Gloria's pocket watch again.

Sure enough, the dead woman's name was there in the address book: Janet Dodds, late thirties, a longtime member of Ferry's custodial staff. Everyone on the ship received a standard income; necessary jobs came with wages on top of that. Custodians were among the most highly paid of all, along with Medical staff, teachers, and Librarians.

I scrolled through the notes. Gloria's written conversations with Janet went back at length, but they didn't appear to be social. They were full of references to Empyrean Designs. I brought up the infobank portal and poked a little further. It seemed Empyrean was a company Gloria and Janet had formed—and it stretched back nearly two hundred years.

Suddenly it seemed vital to find out precisely how Janet had died. Natural, accident, or something more sinister? The timing was enormously dodgy.

I found I rather misliked the idea of walking around wearing the body of a potential murderer.

I found the dead woman—where else?—in the bathroom.

The bathtub was the standard diamond-glass scoop that rose and sank into the floor, to provide everything from a spill lip for a shower to a full tub for a relaxing soak. Janet Dodds had raised hers to its full height, filled it full of memory liqueur, and then drowned in it.

Or so it appeared.

The rainbow swirl of liquids had preserved her like a damselfly in amber, a look of awe and wonder on her face. I recognized some of the colors: the soft pink of a sunrise, the greens of walks through woods in spring. Miss Dodds's thick red hair drifted in curls around her like something out of John Singer Sargent, and her hands were raised softly to the surface of the liquid as though reaching out to cradle something that would vanish if grasped too tightly.

It was all very pretty and very tragic, and could not have been more obviously staged.

It was the prettiness of it that convinced me: this was a romantic's notion of death by overindulgence. None of the graceless poses or unpleasant smells that usually came with corpses. People who drowned in memories also forgot where they were: they splashed and thrashed and spilled liquors all over in the throes of their final confusion. But the bathroom around me was pristine—as if it had been cleaned up, wiped down, and presented to a jury like a painting in an exhibition.

We detectives had seen a great deal of this kind of death in the early days, when people were still adjusting to their new reality of life on board ship. The temptation toward consciousness-altering experiences was very human, and the existence of the Library meant even fatal experiments didn't stay fatal. Our bodies were temporary—at least until that distant day of planetfall, when we'd pick one to keep until real, permanent death overcame us.

But being temporary was not the same as being disposable. And that was how Janet had clearly been treated: as something to be gotten rid of. A nonmystery with all the bows tied up nice and neat for whoever was first to find her.

It was an affront to any detective's soul, even if they weren't—possibly—walking around with the hands that had done the deed.

Murder had happened before on the *Fairweather*. We were all still human, after all. The first century of the crossing had seen several famous incidents: a fraudster, a jealous lover, a brawl in a pub that went too far. But murder trials were quite different when the victim could be brought in to testify in court—or when the shipmind could subpoena the killer's own memories as evidence. One victim had even been able to name her murderer, since she'd realized she'd been poisoned and managed to make it to the Library and update her memory-book in the last instants before her body's death.

And since killing someone no longer removed them permanently but still came with many of the old punishments, the payoff was generally not deemed worth the effort.

Unless someone had come up with something clever to shift that calculus.

It was a thought to send a chill through all my borrowed bones.

Maybe Gloria's not a killer, I thought. Grasping at straws, but it helped shake off the paralysis. *Perhaps the two of them were just having a little fun, and something went wrong, and Gloria panicked. Perhaps some third party was involved.*

And after all, Miss Dodds could be restored from her memory-book.

Couldn't she?

What was it Ferry had said? I'd been put in Gloria's body because someone had erased my book from the Library. What if other books had been damaged as well? By the storm, or by sabotage?

Those questions would be the first ones I'd ask once Ferry was, well, sober again.

In the meantime, I could start pulling threads on the other mystery: the secret copy of my mind that Ferry had brought forward when my real copy was erased.

And I knew precisely who was to blame.

FAR MORE AWE-INSPIRING THAN THE STARS, to my mind, was the view of the *Fairweather*'s heart.

Vast round windows in both bow and stern, like the domes of some sideways cathedral, now flickering with the green-and-purple auroras of magnetic disturbances. Ramps and lifts up and down between decks, abandoned from the storm and the lateness of the hour. The diamond patterns of the metal railings, turning shadows into stripes. Doors both simple and ornate, flanked by planters and chairs. Flats and home shops and small cafés, vanishing into the distance, an entire small city flowering as it sped through the great dark nothing.

This little world was made for us, for humans, had been carefully designed and painstakingly built to be a refuge and a comfort on the long journey from our old home to our new one.

And of course the Greenway, the hydroponic garden that wound up the middle of it all. The soaring trees that shielded the towers of planting tiers had filled out a little in the past two years, stretching toward the great solar lamps pendant from the ceiling. Someone with a very green thumb had succeeded in making a little lawn of velvet moss that bounded the whole of the garden and made it look like an emerald set into a silver cuff. Pretty, and practical, too—all that greenery dampened sound and filtered the air into something that smelled almost natural. Like a little bit of Old Earth we could enjoy without having to riffle through fading remembrances for it.

It was all empty now, silent and dark as space itself. I'd never seen it like this before. Even at night there had always been the sounds of cocktail bars and jazz bands and people working late shifts to keep the whole machine humming. The occasional midnight cycle races, riders spinning by in descending spirals and taking the corners at ludicrous speeds. But now all those ramps were empty, their lengths arcing between decks like the ribs of some great interstellar beast, borne along on nighttime tides.

I shivered and walked as fast as I dared to Ruthie's apartment.

My nephew had apparently moved into a sober, suspiciously respectable neighborhood on Forward Port Five, all tall two-story apartments with upper balconies. This deck was on the same level as in the canopy of the Greenway's trees, maple and apple and oak stretching out just past the railing like welcoming arms. It would be pretty in the daylight; now, with the solar lamps dimmed in artificial night, the tree branches looked eerie and skeletal and cast grasping fingers over the empty balcony above my head.

I felt like a witch roaming a wood on some Hallows' Eve as I raised a hand and rapped sharply on the door of Ruthie's flat.

It took several more knocks before the door creaked open. Slim pale hands rubbed at bleary eyes and shoved errant brown curls away from a tall forehead.

When the *Fairweather* was first constructed, back on the planet we barely recalled, I'd thought the journey an awful idea even before I learned Ruthie was one of the primary minds behind it. I had enough trouble with the sea crossing on my annual voyage from New York to London to visit my sister, Alexandra, and her son; you'd never catch me cruising across the stars. But then Alex had died, and Ruthie and I had only each other—and when he'd asked me to take her berth, I hadn't the heart to say no.

Stay behind and be all alone, while my nephew contended with a ship full of strangers, any one of whom might be up to who knew what sort of malice or mayhem? Unthinkable.

I smiled at him now, because despite the murder and the

borrowed body and the drunken shipmind, it was good to see his face again in person. "Hello, Ruthie."

"Yes?" Those familiar eyes blinked again, then focused. "It's Miss Vowell, isn't it?"

Wait: *Ruthie* knew Gloria?

Just how far did this web of deception stretch?

Abruptly, my plans made a pivot. Deception might be safer, until I had a better sense of the situation. "I'm so sorry to bother you so early, Mr. Talmadge—"

"And during a magnetic storm, too," Ruthie mumbled.

"—but I wasn't sure where else to go." At least that much was true. I put a hand on the doorframe and tried to make my face look pleading.

Good heavens, what did Gloria's face even *look* like? Should have checked in a mirror earlier.

Ruthie only stood there, rumpled and blinking.

"May I come in?" I asked eventually.

"Oh! Yes, I suppose so," he said, and pulled the door wider. "John?" he called out. "Company."

Did Ruthie live with someone now? Another new development since my retirement to the Library. I smiled what I hoped was an apologetic smile and turned to face the stranger as he emerged from the bedroom above.

He was tall and dark-haired, and his eyes had a gentle fold on the lids. He wore pyjamas with a deep blue stripe, covered with a dressing gown cinched tight and tied as precisely as any cravat. "Miss Vowell," he said in a voice like brushed steel. "May I get you something to drink?"

Ruthie beamed, pride coming off him like solar radiation. "Of course you'll be familiar with John's talents as a memory artist."

"Of course," I murmured. Ruthie's always loved a cocktail—no surprise to hear he'd fallen for a cocktail maker.

When our long voyage had first been planned, or so Ruthie was fond of telling me, one of the major questions had been: How do we handle the discrepancy between the short life of the body and the long life of the mind that the journey will require? The Founding Board didn't want to lose any of the passengers' experience and knowledge, however trivial it seemed—but you could only fit so much of that experience in a single human brain before it began to overflow its banks.

The memory liquors had been Ruthie's answer. Memories of Earth, the kind we couldn't make on board the *Fairweather,* sorted by type and distilled into distinct colors and flavors. You could mix them like any cocktail, and with the same ratio of success to failure—certain flavors of experiences went together, while others clashed. I'd once tasted Ruthie's idea of combining the roar of artillery with the coo of a baby's first laugh: he had tried to call it artistic and avant-garde, but you might as well have mixed gin and rum and poured it over olives instead of ice. A disaster on every conceivable level.

Any memory artist worth his license should be well aware of how to combine various types for best effect.

I decided this would be as good a gauge of this John's mettle as any. "I'll have a summer storm, please."

John nodded easily and walked to the cabinet in the corner, where glass and liquid sparkled in a rainbow of hues and an orchestra of shapes.

I settled myself in an armchair, bouncing a little to test the stuffing, taking the opportunity to examine the room. Tasteful furnishings in soft and pleasing neutrals. Small silver art pieces on the mantel over the glow of the retromat, and a soothing landscape print in an unostentatious frame. A glossy caramel-colored piano in one corner, with sheets of music whose disarray argued for lamentable frequency of use. A desk in the same color wood, a corkboard full of paper notes and calendar dates, and—ah! A newspaper clipping with a photo of several men, including John himself. Gloria's twenty-seven-year-old eyes were sharp enough to pick his name out of the fine print of the caption: JOHN PENGELLY.

The only garish colors were the memory liquors, and even those had been harmoniously arranged in spectrum order.

"Are you sure Mr. Talmadge lives here?" I asked. "I don't see any novelty cocktail shakers or cartoons of humorously shaped vegetables."

John shuddered. "And you never will, madam." He was currently pouring something long and lilac into a simple silver shaker. A dusting of gold shimmer, a dab of white mist, shaken and poured over ice in a highball glass. He set it on the table beside me with a knowing smile, then returned to mix something else for himself and my nephew. His own was deep amber, Ruthie's a wretched blue. "To the future," John said.

"To the future," we chorused, as was traditional.

I settled my back against the chair—really it was perfectly comfortable, damn the man—and took an experimental sip.

I'd challenged him and expected he would respond with a show of force . . . but it turned out this memory artist had subtlety.

That would be the first and last time I would underestimate John Pengelly.

First to my senses came the remembered scent of ozone, metallic over the bright, sweet flavor of grass warmed by sunlight. Then clouds built up into thunderheads, white piles turning slowly charcoal as the chill of the rain poured down. Stark flashes of lightning that briefly blinded me, as wind tossed my wet hair back from my face and thunder rumbled a bass note I felt deep in my chest. I was still buzzing with it as the storm moved on down the hill and leaves and petals scattered about me, wind blowing the droplets into mist, the taste of petrichor fresh and tart on my tongue.

Then even that faded, and I was back in Mr. Pengelly and Ruthie's oh-so-tasteful parlor.

My nephew was all attention and anxious query, sitting up in his chair like a human exclamation point—but his partner waited comfortably, stoic and serene.

For a moment, I could barely breathe. I had memories of Old Earth, same as most people on the *Fairweather*. But those were memories stored in the mind—visions and echoes and impressions, muffled by distance and softened by time. Something more like dreams, at this point.

This had felt like the kind of memory the body carried. Athletics, musical training, trauma, and ecstasy all left invisible marks on flesh. It was why blank bodies never stayed blank, and why there was always an adjustment period after a reembodiment. It was one thing for a memory cocktail to call up a feeling from my own past—the tempest I'd seen in the country when I was only twenty-two, for instance, which was usually what happened when I ordered a summer storm.

This cocktail had been not an echo, but an experience. For a moment my body had been convinced I was really there, physically present, with the gravity of a solid planet holding me down and a true wind sharp on my cheeks.

Mr. Pengelly set his own drink aside and folded careful hands. "Now, madam—perhaps you could tell us who you really are."

* * *

OH DEAR.

"I told you," I said, mind racing, "I'm Gloria Vowell."

"I've met Gloria Vowell several times," Mr. Pengelly said, "and never once has she ordered anything but a city sunrise."

Ruthie gasped. "Crimes Committed!"

"I don't think so, my dear," John said, with a shake of his head.

I leaned forward, not yet ready to give in. "So because I ordered a different drink I must be a different person? Are all bartenders so philosophical?"

"Only the exceptional ones. Answer the question, please."

"And if I refuse?"

He said nothing but moved one hand to the arm of his chair, the tip of a corkscrew jutting from his fingers and catching the light in a very speaking kind of way.

"Interesting," I breathed. "Where did you say you learned your craft, Mr. Pengelly?"

Ruthie interrupted: "Leave the poor man alone, Aunt Dorothy."

John started.

I stared.

Ruthie blinked at both of us above the rim of his cocktail glass. He looked as surprised as either of us, to be frank.

I bowed to the inevitable with a sigh. "He's right. I am his Aunt Dorothy. And since we're being frank, I should tell you both that the fact that I'm walking around in someone else's body is all my nephew's fault."

Ruthie automatically sputtered in protest—unfortunate, as he was trying to take a drink at the time. He wiped blue mist from his cheeks and stared at me in horror. "You can't really be Aunt Dorothy! You're a good ten years younger than me!"

I pinched the bridge of my nose. "It's just the body, Ruthie."

"Oh! Oh. Yes, I suppose it—it's just . . . You just always *feel* older, is all."

"I shall take that as a compliment."

"Gosh." He took a longer, steadier gulp of whatever blue nightmare Mr. Pengelly had made for him. "Have you been Gloria this whole time?"

"Of course not! I woke up in her body two hours ago. Ferry was—well, Ferry was drunk." I narrowed my eyes. "Ferry also said something about a secret backup, and a script that executes whenever a detective's book gets erased."

My nephew's blush was as good as a confession. "I'm sure I don't know what you mean."

I sighed. "Ruthie, you are easily the worst liar I've ever encountered."

"I shall take that as a compliment."

I changed tack. "How do you know Miss Vowell?"

"Well, she's a member of the Antikythera Club, of course."

I shook my head. "Of course."

The Antikythera Club: Ruthie's collection of bright sparks and brilliant minds. Scriptwriters, chemical wunderkinds, mathematical geniuses, inventors of all kinds—they all seemed to gather together in the well-padded bar to debate ideas, make scientific breakthroughs, and debauch themselves. They took in cocktails, fine wines, and rich dinners—and they exported trouble in previously undreamt-of ways.

I was not surprised to hear they were involved in all this. It was only a wonder they hadn't gotten anybody killed.

Or—maybe they finally had. Janet Dodds's death still needed explaining, after all. "Tell me about this emergency script. It's important," I added when Ruthie tried to protest again.

My nephew's mouth turned downward as his mood abruptly clouded. "It was meant to protect you, Aunt. After

Celia—after the first magnetic storm, I worked double shifts all week trying to figure out a way to keep anything like that from happening again. We've got a policy of battening down during storms now, after a few of them knocked power offline in a few places. People have come to treat them as a sort of holiday. We lock down everything on the top decks—the Library and Medical and all that—and everyone stays home until things blow over. And Ferry usually takes, well, a bit of a nap while it happens. It's a little hard on the poor thing. Alice figured out some improvements to the shielding, which helped—but we thought it was best to have several methods. Safety in redundancy, you know."

"So you made a copy of my memory-book. For all the ship's detectives or only me? How about the Board of Directors—are they doubled as well?" I leaned forward, hands gripping my knees as I followed the implications. "Even if you only copied those two groups, that's still a lot of extra memory-books. Where are you storing them?"

Ruthie squirmed. "The Board is always doubled, and always has been. We just don't make that knowledge public," he said. "So adding the ship's detectives didn't actually take *that* much added shelf space. It was more an extension of an existing protocol than a whole new project."

"Your nephew pushed for it," Mr. Pengelly put in softly. "Not only because of Celia. But because he'd come close to losing you, and it was tearing him to pieces."

I blinked.

"Here now, John," my nephew harrumphed. It was a completely unthreatening, thoroughly aspirational sound, like a puppy trying to learn how to swear convincingly. His ears had gone pink again, and his eyes went everywhere they could to avoid meeting mine. "There's no call to go embarrassing a fellow by telling his aunt his actual feelings."

Mr. Pengelly almost smiled.

"And anyway, it *worked*," Ruthie said, eyes going wide again. "Ferry put you in a passenger's body because your original book *was* erased!" He stood and paced, hands clasped behind his back. "Has our shielding broken down? Was there something different about this last storm? Or—"

He stopped, and did meet my eyes this time, and I could clearly see the thought go through his brain: *Or has someone done it on purpose?*

"Oh, Aunt Dorothy," he whispered. "I think it *is* all my fault."

Five seconds prior, I would have said the same. But he sounded so despondent that I bit back my automatic agreement. "How so?" I asked instead.

He tugged anxiously at the cuffs of his robe. "Last month, Alice and I were in the club, having a cozy drink after a shift. We'd just finished installing the last of the newest piece of shielding—rather fun, actually, it's a type of polarized diamond-glass, where—"

Mr. Pengelly coughed gently.

Ruthie caught himself and sent his partner an indulgent look. "All right, I won't tire you with the details. But we were talking about the things we'd learned about certain kinds of light affecting the Library, and how you could theoretically create a tool in a standard retromat that would let someone erase an entire memory-book. Alice was thinking it might come in handy someday—she's got a bug in her ear about how often people write over the books, and that it might be better practice to erase them in between backups. Less chance of data corruption, she says, though I'm not convinced." He plucked a piece of fluff on the knee of his pyjama bottoms. "And we were arguing quite loudly about it by this point, and I'm sure I heard a door open or close nearby, which means someone could have heard us. We laughed it off as Crimes Committed, but now . . . I wonder."

"What kind of tool? Something like this?" I pulled the torch out of Gloria's trouser pocket.

Ruthie took it gingerly and flicked the switch: it shone a sinister red-orange, and his cheeks went pale. "Yes, this would do it. But you'd also need a reflective surface of some kind—"

"Such as a mirror?" I held out the small compact as well.

Ruthie's eyes widened in horror. "Aunt Dorothy, what have you done?"

"Not me," I said. "Gloria had these in her pockets."

"*Gloria* erased your memory-book?" Ruthie looked aghast. "The club secretary will have to be informed!"

John coughed again, almost as if he weren't laughing.

"We don't know what Gloria's done, if anything," I said. "But there is something else..." And I explained about Janet Dodds's corpse.

"I was heading up to the Library today anyway, once the storm had passed," Ruthie said at the end of this. His eyes briefly looked sadder and older than they ever had. "And to think, I was so excited that the memory-books would finally be safe from harm. Two years' worth of work, and for what?"

"Think of it this way," I replied. "Now you have the chance to find a new way to protect people. Not just your aunt, either."

Ruthie perked up, as he always did when there was a puzzle or a problem for his mind to take apart. "I suppose you're right. Meet me there, at least?"

"As soon as I can," I promised. The last sip of my drink vanished with a cool breeze and the taste of rain. "For now, I think it's time Gloria's body found its way home."

THE SHIPMIND COULD NEVER REALLY GO ENtirely to sleep—it still had to make sure we didn't drift into a black hole or some such—so the journey to Gloria's flat was punctuated by sounds and signs that indicated Ferry was still suffering from the magnetic storm's effects. Lifts wheezed with effort, stairwell lights flickered, and hollow metallic moans made ghostly echoes in the plumbing and the vents.

I had decided to walk, partly to give myself time to sort out my thoughts, but also because in the blink of an eye I had gone from a dying body wracked with pain to one that was hale and hearty and a mere twenty-seven, and I needed some time to get used to it.

How strange to stride forward as fast as I pleased, and feel only the pleasant ache of working muscle instead of sharp pains and sluggish disobedience. It took me longer than I liked until I felt comfortable testing this body's limits and strength. My prior body's legs hadn't even been responding to my commands at the end.

It had not been the first time I'd experienced disability—blank bodies were identical in theory but not in practice, because manufacturing humans was still extraordinarily complex and some variation was inevitable—but the end of my last lifetime had seen the longest and most painful decline of all my three-plus centuries. The experience had left deeper scars than usual on the part of me that continued after that body was gone.

I left the stairwell—trusting the lift while Ferry was sleeping seemed like just the sort of brilliant decision that would get me trapped between decks—and made my way past all the bijoux cafés. Plenty of passengers converted the front rooms of their living quarters to shops and restaurants, and over the centuries with all of us living and dying and moving around, similar types had begun to cluster into something like Old Earth neighborhoods.

Aft Starboard Twelve was a much more bohemian address than I'd expected from a bank clerk. Especially one prone to suits of sober gray like the one I'd spent the night in. But maybe this was merely how Gloria dressed for her job, and in her leisure hours she preferred soft sweaters and printed skirts and cigarettes packed with more than tobacco. Presently, the aromas of tea and espresso and retromatted pastries floated warmly on the air, beckoning to the bleary-eyed folk who would soon be awake and about when the storm was done. Bookstores and art supply stores filled the spots between cafés, and every corner had a small nook stage that would eventually showcase musicians playing for tips or professional bands hired by local shop owners.

I reached Gloria's address, and to my surprise—and no small delight—it turned out the woman lived in a yarn store.

All at once I remembered the arthritis in my hands was gone now, too.

A thrill, but I tamped it down. These hands were only borrowed—I'd see about getting a new body of my own once Ferry was awake, but until then, best not to disturb Gloria's life more than was absolutely necessary.

Besides, I'd never knit with a murderer's hands, and I wasn't about to start now.

The idea made me pause. Gloria's thumbprint would open the door with no trouble, but going inside felt uncomfortably thievish. I told myself firmly there was no point in changing all the biometrics if we would only have to change them back in a day or two.

For a while I simply stood there, in a stolen body, on someone else's threshold, wondering how it had come to this.

Then the habits of my career—and my own considerable nosiness, let's be frank—came to the fore.

I opened the door and flicked on the lights and nearly expired from pleasure.

Was there anywhere better than a yarn store? And this one was exceptional, just organized enough to feel controlled but full of enough color and texture to be a riotous sensual feast. From the threshold I was lured forward by delicate skeins of mohair and long twists of tweed, soft woolens and shimmering silks in everything from vivid rainbows to elegant neutrals. Needles in various sizes, straight and circular, filled a row of glass jars on the wall, commodities that doubled as decor.

And dear heavens, the finished and blocked projects! A blanket folded on top of a set of shelves showed off an arbor's worth of floral squares. Socks in cables and lace. And pinned up high in pride of place, a lace mohair shawl knit in two shades of green, which looked like the long curling leaf of a fern.

I was across the room before I realized, staring up at the stitches. The pattern was unfamiliar to me, the technique a puzzle that made my hands itch to learn how it would feel in the making. Either it was new since my retirement, or Gloria had written it herself.

If so, Gloria was absolutely a genius.

"You've got some nerve, haven't you."

I started and spun round.

A golden goddess was descending the stairs, glaring at me like death herself.

My detective's eye helpfully catalogued the details. Hair whose honey-blond waves were ruffled by restless sleep. A filmy robe and nightgown in aqua, one of those layered ensembles you couldn't really see through but the thought that you *might* be able to kept you entranced and thirsty for a glimpse. Sharp cheekbones, soft lips, and hazel eyes with hints of green. Beautiful eyes, brimming over with hurt, and relief, and rage at the first two.

My mouth went dry and my pulse started a tango. Dizzy, I wondered if this was my own reaction or some holdover response of Gloria's. It had been a very long time since I had been this hammered by pure physical attraction.

Of course, it had been a very long time since I'd last been twenty-seven, so.

"Well," the goddess demanded, "what have you to say for yourself?"

Heat flooded my cheeks as reality sidled up and elbowed me like a coconspirator. Stupid, stupid Dorothy—I'd assumed Gloria's unmarried status meant she lived alone. Obviously, I'd assumed wrong.

Obviously, this was a disaster.

Hazel eyes blazed at me, waiting for my response.

I could see the whole dance play out before me: the

balletic choreography of dodges, half-truths, and outright lies I'd have to deal out like face cards if I wanted to keep this woman from realizing that I was not who she thought I was. And then, once Gloria was back to herself, the choice she'd have to make of either letting this moment go unexplained and unremarked—or revealing the truth and compounding the pain of betrayal with the revelation of my deception.

I was far, far too old and tired for such nonsense.

"I'm so sorry," I said instead, making her stare. "But Gloria's not here."

Her eyes began to shimmer with tears, and I silently cursed my clumsy tongue. "How can you be so cruel?" she said, plaintive and wavering. "You know how I worry on the nights you don't come home."

"But I didn't—"

"I suppose you'll try to convince me you slept at the Antikythera Club again?"

"No—well, maybe, but I—"

"And that this has nothing to do with Janet?"

The name was all but spat out, the woman's tone topful of vitriol, the dead woman clearly a sore point of long standing.

My detective's soul flung itself at that target like an arrow. "Janet's dead."

Those gemlike eyes softened briefly. It looked like—regret?—but as soon as I'd named it, it was gone. "I truly am sorry to hear that," she said, voice trembling. "I know you think I'm only jealous—*Violet, you harpy, stop imagining things,* I think were your words—but truly I bore her no ill will for her own sake. I know you've known each other since First Century. I only . . ." She bit her lip, and I tamped down an unreasonable rush of lust to see her sharp teeth press into that full pink curve. "I only wanted to feel as though I were of equal importance to your life in *this* century, is all. It's embarrassing when someone you love would rather be shelved with their business partner than with you."

She was right: sharing space in the Library was something people did with romantic partners, not financial ones. This woman clearly had more of the answers I needed. "Look, is there someplace we can sit for a bit while I explain? It might take some time."

She—Violet—sighed. "If you must," she said. "We might as well have tea while you spin whatever lies you've dreamt up this time."

I followed her into a smart and sleek little kitchen, all silver and blue, and took a seat in a tall thin-legged chair by a café table with an enameled mosaic top. The woman went to the autochef, and I took the opportunity to surreptitiously scour Gloria's pocket watch for her name.

Violet St. Owen, current body-age thirty-one, yarn store proprietor and knitting designer. I'd have loved to delve more deeply into her published patterns—that fern shawl was something truly spectacular and I wanted it desperately—but just then Miss St. Owen—Violet—came back with two steaming cups. The tea turned out to be Earl Grey with lemon, honey, and just the right amount of bergamot.

It occurred to me, as I took another, longer sip, that Gloria was a fool.

The autochef, like the retromat it was based on, could produce anything the operator remembered, precisely as the operator remembered it. But memories were extremely dodgy blueprints, and a cook's momentary lack of concentration could lead to dishes that were more fiasco than fine cuisine.

Violet clearly had better-than-average recall, and a precision of focus that a ship's detective was in a better-than-average position to appreciate.

I let one more sip of tea warm my throat before I began to speak. "There was an—incident—last night . . ." I began. I told her everything: Ferry being drunk, Janet being drowned, me being a ship's detective. I told her my name and that she could look me up in the infobank. I left out Ruthie's theories about how to erase memory-books—the fewer people who heard about that, the better—but told her his name and that she could look him up, too. "And now there's one death to solve, and maybe other crimes committed along the way," I finished, "and it would be very helpful if you could manage to believe me."

Throughout this recitation, Violet's face had gone icier and icier. When I asked her to believe me, her eyes flashed cold as Arctic lightning. "I must admit," she said, every syllable sharp as glass, "you've gone to quite a bit more trouble with this lie than you usually do. It's a minor masterpiece, in fact. Should I feel flattered?"

"It's the truth!" I insisted. Frustration burned in my throat and put a fist in my gut. Ferry could confirm my story once the ship was awake—but the storm was due to last for hours yet, and I was growing more and more impatient, feeling stuck and stymied at every turn.

Violet's mouth pinched. "Is this because I wouldn't loan you that money? Honestly, Gloria, that level of borrowing— it's just irresponsible. I own a business, too, you know, and I know that kind of debt isn't good to have on the books."

"No, it's . . ." My voice trailed off as my brain caught up. Gloria had been taking on loans for Empyrean Designs? Money was still the root of many crimes, even on a ship where everyone's needs were seen to. I'd been planning on looking into the company, of course, but now I had a better idea of what I'd be looking for.

Violet was still watching me, suspicion in her expression but an oddly eager light in those hazel eyes. As though she were just waiting to discount the next thing I said, whatever it was.

As though she *needed* not to believe the truth.

Following that hazy instinct, I leaned forward, watching her closely. "You're right," I said, as dolefully and sincerely as I could manage. "I've been beastly. What can I do to make it up to you?"

Surprise, quickly and quietly hidden—and a flash of cunning that I wouldn't soon forget.

Violet dropped her gaze—a convenient gesture—and sighed, and set her teacup aside. "I'm tired, Gloria. Tired of the lies and the late nights, and all the arguments." She plucked the cups from the table and stood to put them in the washer. Over her shoulder, gold hair cascading down blue silk, she said: "I think it's time we agreed to be done. I'll have your things packed up and will let you know when you can come get them."

My jaw fell open. Had I really gotten Gloria *jilted*?

If what Violet said was true, then Gloria certainly deserved it—but it felt a little unfair that it was landing on me and not her. The first woman I'd been attracted to since Celia, and the first thing she did was break up with me.

I could have laughed, if it didn't smart so badly.

Thirty seconds later I was outside the flat again, my head spinning and my stomach aching with tea and too much confusion. My soul felt as rumpled as my suit, which was beginning to look much the worse for wear after a night with no sleep and too many questions.

Violet shut off the yarn store lights, and it felt like being cut adrift on an endless sea.

So I asked myself, as a detective: What would a newly single Gloria do in this circumstance? Where would she find refuge after a row like that?

One place leapt instantly to mind.

IN THE MIRROR BEHIND THE BAR IN THE
Antikythera Club, Gloria's face stared back at me like an
accusing ghost. Peaked eyebrows, dark hair, and skin like
new parchment: pale with gold undertones. There was a scar
on her lip from frequent chewing, and lashes so lush you
couldn't help but envy them.

I scowled, and it felt like the mirror image was blaming
me for shattering two strangers' hearts.

"That does it," I murmured to John as he mixed maples
in fall with the scent of a bonfire and poured the results into
a highball glass. At some point this body would need food
of some kind, but for now all I was craving was something
to take the imaginative edge off. "I'm getting reembodied.
Just as soon as I untangle this mess. Hopefully by the end
of the day."

"Aren't we confident," he murmured back, but softened it with one of those almost-smiles.

I drank, and let a dream of autumn fall around me like silent leaves. I was forming a solid suspicion about my nephew's beloved, but that could wait.

I turned to ogle my surroundings.

In three centuries on board the *Fairweather* I'd never been to the Antikythera Club. This would be a brand-new memory, freshly made. Something to be savored.

I was perched on a stool at the long mahogany bar, beneath a dazzling dangle of globe lights. Behind me were a flock of half-circle chairs in green velvet, slowly filling up now that the storm was officially past. A long chalkboard on one wall was being filled with letters and numbers by a pair of young women, who murmured to each other as they worked and occasionally stopped to erase and rewrite sections. A round older man with richly dark skin and a neat beard was reading in the far corner, pages turning and his plate of bacon and beans going cold at his elbow.

On the left- and right-hand walls, metal rays glinted to show the way to other areas of the club: I could glimpse a library through one double doorway and an observation room through the other, a bank of diamond-glass windows stretching from floor to ceiling, with a scattering of telescopes to hand for spotting comets, nebulae, and passing planets.

It was luxurious without being fussy, cozy without being cramped, and I never wanted to leave. The chair in the corner nearest the bar would be perfect for knitting and eavesdropping. "Do you have any open member slots?" I asked John.

"I'll bring you the application form," he replied.

I hid my next question behind the rim of my highball glass, in case my lip trembled. "Has Ruthie told you about Celia?"

John's gaze was direct but not accusing. "He's mentioned her name. I haven't pressed him for the full story."

I took a sip and let memory warm its way down my throat, bracing me. "In my last lifetime, I had a wife. We'd met on ship and married in the space of a year, as stupidly in love as if we were teenagers who didn't know any better. We used to joke we were doing things the wrong way round: we'd met as old women, and only afterward got to be young together again." Oh, the pang of that still ached. You'd think there'd be a scar there by now for protection, but apparently I wasn't so healed as that. "The years and the lifetimes went by—until two years ago. I was having trouble walking, but that had happened in other embodiments of mine and I wasn't too troubled. But Celia . . . Celia was having memory problems. Especially from more recent years—the old memories, from Earth and childhood, those were well ingrained and stayed steady. But later things were fuzzier. Including her memories of our relationship. She refreshed her memories from the Library once every few weeks, but it was a bit wearing on both of us in the moments when she forgot."

"That sounds very hard," John replied gently.

"Well, perhaps, but I thought it would only be hard temporarily," I returned. "We had a thousand years to look forward to. I wasn't about to throw that away for mere convenience's sake. And maybe I should have pushed harder for her to get reembodied sooner—but she resisted, and it felt callous of me to push. And then the first magnetic storm happened. And her book in the Library got damaged. Severely."

John shook his head.

I took another sip of autumn. "We uploaded her from her body as soon as her memory-book was repaired, then decanted her into a new body so she could form memories properly again—but she'd lost so much. She barely remembered who I was, and it felt—it felt like taking advantage, to stay with someone who had to take our whole romance on faith. Oh, she said she believed me, but . . ." I sighed. "It wasn't enough. I wanted it to be, but I couldn't make it feel like enough. It felt like I was married to a ghost—or she was, I couldn't decide. Either way, it wasn't any decent way for people to live."

"So rather than get reembodied yourself, you—retired?"

"Which was also supposed to be temporary," I said, my

voice dry as dead leaves. "But every time my turn came up and Ferry asked if I was ready to come back, I said no." I toyed with the edge of the paper coaster. "And I ended up here anyway."

"Fate loves its little jokes."

"Ruthie does, too."

"He wouldn't consider this a joke. At all."

I peered at him and waited.

His mouth was stern but in a kindly way, his hands steady as he turned a retromatted lime into zest and garnishes. "A few months after I met your nephew, there was a particularly bad magnetic storm. He was quite shaken, and ended up telling me the part about it being possible to impose one person's memory-book on someone else's body." The little paring knife flickered against the peel. "The idea has rather weighed on my mind. It feels . . . ripe for a very specific kind of abuse, in the wrong hands."

"I agree with you," I said. "Ruthie, bless him, often overlooks the implications of his theories and solutions."

"But you do not."

"No—I consider it my job to be suspicious and mistrustful of people, as a rule. Even when it's my own nephew, whom I love." I sighed. "It is my auntly responsibility, you see."

He inclined his head, rinsing citrus pulp away and wiping his hands dry on the dark cloth at his waist. "I quite understand, Mrs. Gentleman. I would hope any aunt of mine would do the same."

"Do you have any family on board ship?"

"A scattering of uncles and cousins. No aunts. We meet up once a year or so to commiserate about it."

Despite myself, I snorted a laugh. "Yes, you can tell he missed me by how horrified he was when I reappeared." Something from that earlier conversation bobbed back to the surface of my mind. "What does 'Crimes Committed' mean?"

John *tsk*ed. "Nothing. At least—nothing real. I'm reasonably certain it started as a joke here in the club. Members are always theorizing wildly on whatever subjects interest them, but not always in ways the Board is going to put into practice—I don't have to tell you why that is—so I believe they dreamed up a group that would find all those illicit technologies and scientific byways valuable. They call them Crimes Committed, after—well, I suppose it's self-explanatory."

"A shadow council."

"Of a sort, yes."

It certainly wasn't the first time I'd heard such rumors. Humans were remarkably consistent in some ways: they imagined something noble like justice or virtue, and the very next thing they'd think up was its opposite.

Since by now there was no point in trying to maintain anything like an objective distance from Gloria's life, I passed the time by reading her correspondence. Every *I'll be late* message, every *Where are we meeting for dinner,* every *I'm sorry* and *Please answer* and *You can't still be sulking.*

Every note, that is, except the one set that was keyword-encrypted and carefully filed separately from the rest. Not one of Ferry's encryptions, which I could break with a touch as soon as my access was restored. This was artisanal code-work.

Someone didn't want this looked at, and my curiosity sat up and bayed.

I borrowed a pencil and a notebook from John and started a little list of things to look further into. It read:

—*Empyrean Designs business loans*
—*Gloria and Janet shelved together*
—*Memory-book erased: more than one?*

Now I added:

—*Gloria's keyword*

So far, I could see a hundred possible connections between points one and two, and zero connections between those and point three. Hopefully the answers would be found in point four—something like *I, Gloria Vowell, did some crimes and here is why and how.*

I rubbed my aching eyes. Of course it was never that convenient.

But there were still plenty of places left for me to look for answers.

I finished my drink and slipped off the stool.

***

IT WAS A relief to see other passengers walking the decks. Fashions had shifted in the past two years: plaid seemed to have come back into style, and hats were being worn tilted to the left rather than the right.

Ferry's voice sidled into my head. The shipmind finally sounded like itself, stone-sober and deeply abashed. *Hullo, Dorothy. Mr. Talmadge has been explaining to me that apologizing is a traditional thing one does the day after a period of extreme intoxication, and I feel like my first apology should be to you.*

"For what, Ferry?"

I ought to have warned you about the security script in advance. Or at least woken you up and told you what was about to happen. I'm afraid that what with the magnetic storm affecting my—my impulses, for lack of a better term, and in the urgency of a crisis, I simply acted. I'm frightfully sorry, and I promise you it won't happen again.

It might, of course. Ferry knew there were other magnetic storms ahead, and couldn't avoid being affected when that happened. But one had to acknowledge that an effort was being made, and an olive branch extended. "Thank you, Ferry. I'm glad to know I'm your favorite. Because—here's a secret—you're my favorite, too."

A small *hmm* was all the reply. The exact sound that someone would make to cover up the fact that they were blushing.

Ferry unlocked my detective's access—this case was getting messy enough that I needed it, even if we had to relock it once Gloria returned to herself—and I went back to Janet Dodds's apartment. Medical had been through and cleared her old body away, but had left the rest of the place untouched. The ledgers for Empyrean Designs were easy enough to find—but they showed none of the business loans Violet had hinted at. Just a few hundred years of debits and credits, nothing at all unusual. The profits were not a fortune, but they were substantial enough, and reasonably steady for such a volatile industry as fashion.

But when I looked at Empyrean Designs' banking records in the infobank—thank you, Ferry—I noticed something odd.

For the most part, the electronic records matched the handwritten account books exactly. But every thirty to forty years there was a blank. Two to three days of absolutely nothing at all. No interest, no profits, no losses of any kind.

As though someone—a bank clerk, for instance—had been wiping those days from the electronic records.

I'd failed at being Gloria once, then failed at *not* being Gloria. Here's hoping third time really was the charm.

Turned out, it wasn't necessary. The bank tellers were still getting settled at the start of the day, and I was able to slip past to the back where I'd learned the higher-level clerks like Gloria each had one small room to themselves.

Really I was starting to be a little glad I hadn't had to meet her yet. You'd never hear me say it out loud—ship's detectives were supposed to be above that sort of thing—but the more I learned about her, the less I wanted to know.

Gloria's office at Infinity Mutual on Forward Starboard Three was sleek and cold and gray. Just like Gloria's suit—or, I thought privately, like Gloria's heart. Meticulous as a shark in pursuit of what she wanted, heedless of the damage done to anyone else.

I checked the backs of the few photographs on her desk, riffled through the drawers, poked through her computing terminal, and found the Empyrean Designs records I'd already seen—but here, in the security of the bank's offices, I was also able to access their history.

Gloria had indeed been deleting those sections: her access code was all over it, in ways only another bank employee would have been able to see. And I could think of only one reason: these must be the business loans Violet had hinted at.

The Founding Board had taken money very seriously when they set up the *Fairweather*'s financial systems. Past debt should never be a stain on someone's record—so any loans, once repaid, were erased. But that usually showed up as brief single-line gaps scattered over long time periods, as the initial loan and all the subsequent payments quietly vanished and left the rest of the list of payments in and payments out intact.

So either something else was happening that I didn't know about—or the business was taking in loans and then repaying them days later.

But why?

I fingered Gloria's pocket watch. She had saved every note anyone had ever sent her, every snippet of conversation. And backed them up: I'd checked. This was a woman who abhorred a vacuum.

Somewhere, she would have kept a record of those loans. She might have deleted them officially, but she wouldn't let them vanish entirely. They were *hers,* after all.

I was betting they were in those encrypted notes. All I needed was the word that would unlock them.

I tried several basic things—*Violet, Janet, Empyrean, money, crime*—to no avail. Meanwhile, to judge by the increasing volume of people sounds from the hallway and the offices to either side, the ship's population was back to their usual occupations.

And if that was the case, I had a nephew who might prove doubly useful.

I slipped out of the bank, ignoring the looks of surprise and a few calls for attention, and made my way up to the Library.

TO REACH THE LIBRARY I HAD TO TAKE THE
same lift in which I'd awoken, what now felt like a lifetime
ago. The Greenway was now fully lit with fake noon, and I
watched the tall trees shrink as I went up, up, up to the very
highest floor.

I stepped through the narrow foyer into the Library
proper and caught my breath, as I did every time.

It was always daunting to see all ten thousand souls of
the *Fairweather* at once. Tall walls of shelves rose on three
sides of the vast cavern and twisted in a labyrinth across
the floor, with diamond-glass skylights above. These were
covered with the light lavender sheen of shielding film, to
ward off the detrimental effects of radiation and magnetic
storms, but the stars still shimmered there in the depths.

Brighter than the stars, however, was the sparkle of the

more than ten thousand memory-books on those tall shelves. Solid-state glass storage, each volume made of wafer-thin transparent pages threaded with miniature gold circuitry, shimmering with occasional ripples of light in patterns too quick for the eye to follow. All our thoughts had physical form here, all our dreams and hopes and fears, sensations from people and places long past, and visions of all the joys to come.

Immortality, of a sort: every memory every one of us had made for three hundred years—except of death. You could save your mind up to very nearly the end, but you could never bring the memory of dying back with you.

It was probably a kindness, but one couldn't help but wonder.

In the center of it all was the archive station, a wooden desk ringed by a small collection of leather seats and sofas where people could wait when they came to update their memory-books. As I watched, a couple was in the process of getting shelved together. A young person of ambiguous gender was just stepping out of the upload chamber—a glass cube, clear on all sides, with a smaller cube as an entryway on the near side. A young woman in green pressed a kiss to her beloved's cheek before taking their place in the cube.

She placed her fingertips on the glass and gold circuit points, and the Librarian outside reached for the handle that lowered the headpiece. It looked like a small set of organ pipes made of glass, and it took a few adjustments before the woman in the cube reported it rested comfortably snug against her temples.

The Librarian made sure everyone was ready, and pulled the switch.

The cube surface swirled with soft gold ripples as the young woman's mental net was mapped and the data transferred along the cables. A small, swift light burned the patterns layer by layer into the memory-book resting on the stone plate at the archive station.

It took hardly more than a breath, and then the young woman was emerging from the cube and reaching out joyously for her lover's hand.

All the other memory-books began to shift, moved by the sliding shelves beneath them into an iridescent wave like the scales of some enormous fish wriggling in a current, everyone's books sidling over to close the spaces where the two lovers' books had been removed. Two new slots appeared at the bottom right of the shelves, and the refreshed memory-books were placed into those spaces by the archivist. There they would stay, side by side, moving deeper and deeper into the Library, along the twisting rows of shelves, until one or the other or both decided to upload again and move to the front of the queue.

I wondered how many books were currently shelved like

this, in pairs or trios or more, and how many were like mine: solitary, singular, and alone.

I squashed my brief flash of envy, murmured my congratulations as the lovers passed by, and strode forward to speak to the Librarian.

They were able to point me to the aisle where Ruthie was working, a few rows and several turns in.

If you'd only ever seen a duck on land, you would think them terminally awkward: a round, waddlesome, stubby-legged lump of a creature. Only when you saw them floating gently on the mirrored surface of a pond, or coming in for a sleek and skimming landing from the air, would you realize what ducks were truly capable of. You only had to see them in their true element.

Such a creature was Ruthie, who only came into his full potential when surrounded by some immeasurably complex machine. Right now he was sitting half-sprawled on the Library floor, all knees and elbows and loosened tie, arguing with Ferry while a harried assistant sorted gold wires and slender steel tools to one side.

"—no, I understand why you feel embarrassed, but I am telling you, this isn't your fault!"

I cleared my throat.

"Aunt Dorothy." Ruthie sighed and bowed his head. "I know, I ought to have found you earlier—"

"No need to apologize." I sat cross-legged on the floor

beside him. Young joints: so fluid! "I was busy myself. But I'm here now. So: What—" I stopped, staring at the shelf one level up from the floor where we sat. "Ruthie," I said, swallowing hard, "that is more than a little damage."

The entire shelf—the *entire* shelf, a whole row of memory-books—was dark and dull. No sparks, no hum, no light at all. As if one in a string of lightbulbs had burned out—except it wasn't a simple bulb: it was a dozen people's minds.

I went as cold as the black sky above me. "This isn't supposed to be possible! Memory-books are designed to be *permanent*. Thousands of years of stable storage, we were promised!"

"Hundreds of thousands," he agreed morosely. "In theory you could smash them—but you'd only get to one before the shelves would all close up, and an alarm would be sounded. And you're only allowed to know where your own book is shelved, not anybody else's. We learned that lesson back in Century One."

"So then how . . . ?" I waved a wordless hand at the empty, blank books in front of me.

"Theoretically? I've been worrying about exactly this thing, in fact. And I think—it's something about the concentration of light."

I was shaking my head hopelessly. "Give me something other than facts, please, Ruthie."

My nephew's mouth quirked. "Did you ever use a magnifying glass to start a fire, Aunt Dorothy?"

"Not officially." I narrowed my eyes. "Did you?"

His chin lifted at an affronted angle, which in Ruthie language meant: *Absolutely yes, but I will die before I admit it*. "Well, it's like that, but more so. If you see what I mean. The first magnetic storm did it at random—there's probably some astronomical odds against it, but I shall spare you the calculation. But . . . Alice and I were right in our theories, apparently. And now someone's done it."

"Wouldn't the Librarians have noticed someone trying something like that?"

"Normally, yes—but not during a storm. We pull all staff out of the Library during storms, just in case. They can still be a bit unpredictable, and we don't want . . ." He faltered. "We don't want to lose anyone. Which reminds me," he went on, pulling one volume from the shelf. "You'll want to update this as soon as possible, I expect."

He put my own memory-book into my hands. It was very beautiful, very intimate, and very dead. Like a bleached skeleton on the shore, or the ruins of some ancient building. I felt weirdly like I was holding my own skull in my hands.

But it would be far worse to drop it: I gripped it tight, despite my unease. "Will it work?"

"It should. There's no permanent damage that I can find.

And if there is, we'll use Stores to build you another, good as new."

"I'll speak to the Librarians on my way out," I promised. "What about the other books?"

"I have a list of passengers' names, and Ferry's going to reach out to them today and let them know they'll need to update. But, Aunt Dorothy . . . Well, just look."

It didn't take long to see what he meant. Two names from the list leapt out at once: mine—and Gloria Vowell's.

"Does that mean . . . ?" I rasped, mouth dry. I swallowed and tried again. "Gloria's gone?"

Ruthie's face was stricken. "She doesn't have a secondary backup, and her book was on this shelf, three down from yours," he said, pointing to it. Empty, blank, stripped of data, its golden nanowires dull and flat.

I shivered. *Gone.* It was one thing for a body to die: three hundred years of dying and waking up and dying again had meant all of us were more or less used to the idea of bodily death at this point. But for a whole *person* to be gone— all their memories, all their skills, the essence of who they were—for it to be wiped from the record completely, with no way of ever getting it back . . .

My stomach—Gloria's stomach, oh god—lurched. I had one very bad moment when it felt like my body and my mind were fighting to tear apart from each other.

Then Ruthie reached out and grasped my hand. Warm and steady—and familiar. My only family, and the person who knew me best in all the universe. His wide eyes were worried, tired bags beneath them dark as bruises.

I squeezed his hand to reassure him and felt a little better when he smiled with relief.

Having nephews really wasn't always bad. Ruthie might have been an agent of chaos, and his brilliance never seemed to bring him anything but trouble, but he was also a kind heart. Sometimes that was more important than all the rest.

But there was still work to do, and questions to answer. One name had conspicuously *not* leapt out at me from the list. "Ferry, did the lift record anybody entering the Library during the magnetic storm?"

Just one, the ship replied. *A custodial access card.* Custodial staff worked in gloves, so they used cards rather than fingerprints to pass through the various areas on board ship. Ferry's voice was uneasy. *The card belonged to Janet Dodds.*

"But her book wasn't on this shelf?" I remembered what Violet had said: Janet and Gloria had gone to get shelved together.

"Just wait," Ruthie muttered. "I am going to have some very strong things to say to Miss Janet Dodds, believe you me."

"You can't," I replied. "She's dead."

"She's dead *now*," my nephew shot back, "but her memory-book is three shelves away and perfectly functional. She'll be available in a new body by tomorrow morning, and she'd better be prepared! I am planning to be very sharp, Aunt Dorothy. Very sharp indeed!"

"But she was dead before the magnetic storm," I said. "At least, her current body was. So she couldn't have been in the lift."

My nephew blinked. "Then who . . . ? Oh. Gloria, naturally." He scowled. "But why?"

I rose to my feet. "You let me worry about that. I have one more thing to investigate." I bent quickly and kissed his cheek. "Thank you, Rutherford."

He stared up at me in shock and no small amount of concern.

I walked off around the corner before he could recover from his surprise. That was quite enough sincerity for one day. We'd both embarrassed ourselves enough.

I had my memory-book properly updated, persuaded the Librarian to let me see the logbook—where I found just what I expected to find—and took the lift back down to the bank.

Although exhaustion was tugging at my hem like an anxious child, I could feel the last knot of the tangle beneath my hands, and wanted to give it a tug before I lost the thread.

Gloria was gone, and with her went my need to preserve her secrets. Trying not to disturb the patterns of her life had been a struggle, as though I'd fallen into a well and was being pulled drowning into the depths. But now—she was beyond anyone's power to harm.

It was time to upend things.

"THANK GOODNESS," THE HEAD TELLER SAID when I walked back into Infinity Mutual. Her skin was a warm brown, her hair was braided high on her head, and her spectacles were silver and rode low on her long nose. "Mr. Halloran's been waiting nearly half an hour for you."

The name was vaguely familiar from Gloria's contacts. "I don't suppose he said why?"

The teller gave me a sharp look. "Of course not."

"Is this the first time he's visited?"

The sharp look sharpened further, and her eyes grew narrow. "Don't you know?"

I smiled. This might actually be a little bit fun. "To be perfectly frank—no, I don't. I honestly don't remember a thing before this morning." Inspiration came, and with it a wild urge to laugh. For a really good lie, you had to stick to the truth. "I had to restore myself from a much older backup. Two years back, in fact. So there's going to be a lot of loose ends I could use some help with. If you're willing. I know it's a lot to ask, and you have your own work to be getting on with."

The teller stared at me.

I waited.

Apparently some of my sincerity leaked through—and I hadn't lied, not in any way that counted—because she sat back. "All right," she said. "I'll look through the records, if you go in and soothe Mr. Halloran. He seems liable to walk out any minute."

"Thank you"—a quick glance down at her lapel pin—"Mrs. Odita."

"Henry, please," the teller said, with a wry twist of her lips. "I don't know exactly what happened to you in the past two years, but if I were you I'd try to keep it from happening again. This backup of yours is much less irritating."

"So happy to hear it."

Mr. Halloran shot to his feet when I entered the office. "Miss Vowell," he grumbled. He was already a bit red in the face, or what little of it I could see behind the incredible moustaches. He sat when I sat. "I trust there is nothing amiss? Today's the day, after all."

"Today's the day," I agreed pleasantly, as if I had any idea what he meant. "Shall we get started?"

He handed over a transfer chit, made out from Fairweather Central Bank to Empyrean Designs. The crisp egg-shell paper and long strings of account numbers looked official enough to me. I looked at the amount listed in the lower right corner—and my eyebrows nearly caromed right off the top of my face.

He shifted in his chair, leather creaking. "And it's all paid back in two days, yes?"

"Of course," I murmured, throat dry.

"And the interest comes separately?"

Did it? Why? "Of course," I said again, and offered him my most reassuring smile. "Let me get this transfer started, and then I can answer any other questions you might have." I doubted it, but the longer I kept him here the more I was sure to learn. "I'll be right back."

Back in the bank lobby, Henry whistled softly when I slipped the transfer across her desk. "Am I reading that right?" She polished the lenses of her spectacles and looked at it more closely.

"Does Infinity Mutual usually deal in loans that large?"

She snorted. "Hardly. We specialize in small shared corporations, newer cooperatives, that sort of thing. This . . ." She shook her head. "This is money like I haven't seen since before I boarded ship. International investment money." Her mouth pursed. "Frankly, it's a bit indecent."

Privately, I agreed. "So you wouldn't expect Gloria to be able to repay it after two days?"

"Two days?!"

"That's right," I confirmed. "And he mentioned something about interest being paid separately."

Henry latched onto that. "That is absolute nonsense. Why would we—" Her mouth snapped shut, and she suddenly dove for the keys of her computing terminal. She pressed the enter key with a flourish of finality, and sat back. "You're going to want to see this."

I stepped around her desk and peered over her shoulder.

"It's actually rather brilliant, in an appalling kind of way," Henry said.

I shook my head. Figures had never been friends of mine. "No memory, remember?"

Henry's long hand guided me through the lines of numbers. "Infinity Mutual offers higher interest rates on larger business accounts—nothing unusual in that—but unlike larger banks we also offer more frequent compounding of the interest once you're past a certain threshold. This loan amount would mean you're compounding interest once a day. So the first day's interest gets folded into the principal, and earns even more interest on day two. Meaning you've earned this much, in total." She tapped one cell on the screen.

I gaped. The interest alone was almost twice the *Fairweather*'s standard annual income. "So the money comes in, the interest accumulates, and then the money goes back out again. So why keep the interest separate?"

"Well, in the normal course of things, when the money is paid out it erases the original loan. The interest would show up as a profit, and stays visible so it can be tracked and properly taxed. But look—" She indicated an earlier line in the records. "There's an *outgoing* loan already on the books. And it's for precisely the same amount the interest would have earned." She peered up at me. "That cannot be a coincidence."

"Who was the money loaned to?"

She glared up at me. "You."

"Me?" Gloria, she meant. But it was a nasty shock all the same. "Can I ask you to walk me through what that means?"

"You can put in the Central Bank loan money, let it earn two days' worth of interest, and pay the loan back to the source. Large loan vanishes. The interest gets used to pay the earlier, smaller loan. Smaller loan vanishes—and takes the interest record with it. The interest could presumably then be paid to the source as a wholly separate transaction. A personal transfer, if not another bank."

Minus a processing fee for Gloria's time and trouble, no doubt. "Is that . . ."

"Legal? Technically. It appears to be a loophole someone's discovered in the *Fairweather*'s financial systems."

Her mouth was set in stern lines, and her voice hardened. "But it's a loophole that looks a lot like laundering. And it definitely counts as abuse of the General Fund, where the interest is drawn from. I intend to report this to the Crime Committee as soon as possible, Gloria."

"Good," I said fervently.

Mr. Halloran frowned when I returned, with the transfer chit still in my hand, and tucked his gold watch back into his pocket. The gold watch was common enough—anyone could print the parts out from the retromat—but the precise tailoring and cut of his suit spoke loudly of money. A wealthy man who wanted more and was willing to play fast and loose with the rules to get it.

I lowered my voice and tried to look shifty. "I'm so sorry, Mr. Halloran," I muttered, handing him the transfer chit. "They're onto us."

"What?" he said, blanching. "Who?"

I cast a panicked look over my shoulder and let him see it, before bending close. "Do you have somewhere safe to go? Somewhere secret?" Of course he wouldn't—such places didn't exist on the *Fairweather*. I shook my head before he could manage to stop sputtering and answer. "No, it's probably too late for that. One of the others must have talked. There's only one thing to do now."

"What's that?" he wheezed.

"You have to tell the authorities everything and ask for

mercy. Before someone else does it first." I pulled out my notebook and opened it to a fresh sheet. "Here," I said, and wrote the name LELOUP in block letters on the page. "Go to the Detectives' Bureau and ask for this man. Explain everything to him, point by point."

I only wished I could be there in person, when Leloup received this surprise confession like a gift from a secret admirer. Oh, he was going to *hate* it.

Mr. Halloran shoved the paper in a pocket and hastened out of the bank, tugging his hat low over his features in a way that made him look far more suspicious and memorable than if he'd simply walked out with his face bare to the world.

Which confirmed: this whole scam had not been his idea.

It was Gloria's, of course. Who else but a bank clerk could have known about the loopholes she was exploiting? A quick check of Gloria's personal accounts made it clear: she had large gains from unexplained sources at precisely the same times as the gaps in the Empyrean records.

Between the company profits and the shady loan repayments there was quite a staggering amount of funds there—but not a lot of money going back out. No indulgent luxuries, no splashy spending.

Perhaps it was just that she didn't want to draw attention, but it somehow felt more compulsive than that to me.

As though for Gloria the entire purpose of money was to accumulate. A very difficult mindset to hold to on board the *Fairweather*: all personal funds—though not personal objects—returned to the General Fund when a body died. This both prevented individual wealth from spiraling up into absurdity, and incentivized the creation of mutual companies and shared funds, which weren't subject to the same reabsorption. You could get as wealthy as you pleased—you just couldn't do it alone.

And now another pattern slotted into place in my mind: two days' turnaround for a loan was about the same amount of time between when a person died and when their new body was ready for them in Medical.

I pulled up the Empyrean Designs records, with those glaring occasional gaps. Then I pulled up the records of every time Janet Dodds had died in the two centuries since the company's founding.

They lined up precisely, starting at the time of Janet's third body-death after Embarkation.

And there was only one simple way Gloria could have known in advance when Janet was going to die: she'd helped her along.

I poked more closely into Janet's history. One accidental death from a head injury, but otherwise a marked tendency toward heart conditions, with coronary events listed as the cause several times over.

Gloria had been murdering Janet for *centuries*.

To give herself time to launder money, during those two days when nobody else would have access to the shared company's records. A few of those deaths had been suspicious enough to be investigated—I could see the other detectives' reports—but of course they had been ruled out as murder, because a solid motive had never been found. Because the motive came after the murder, not before.

But this time around, Gloria had taken things one crucial step further. She'd killed Janet's body, and then tried to erase Janet's mind.

She'd taken a torch and a mirror and erased the whole shelf, including her own book—and mine—because she knew Janet's book would be beside hers. That was why she'd insisted they be shelved together. It wasn't about the company at all.

And then because she'd erased my book, Ferry had seized her body and imposed my mind over hers at the very moment of her triumph, as she was in the Library elevator fleeing the scene. Erased her mind from her body, while her memory-book lay blank and scorched and empty.

It was a murder-suicide—but only the suicide part would stick.

I sat down hard in the chair behind the desk. The air in the room had gone thin, and I had to suck in several long breaths before the spots cleared from my vision.

After a time, I took out Gloria's pocket watch. The encrypted notes taunted me, the box for the password a fortress wall between me and the only possibility of answers.

I thought about the money in Gloria's account, piling up higher and higher but never used to give her even the smallest amount of pleasure. I thought of her asking Violet for money even though she had so much—perhaps she'd extended her lover the same offer she'd made to Mr. Halloran? I thought of every note she'd saved, every murder she'd committed, every time she'd put her own wants above other people's needs and safety.

I put out a finger and typed a single word: *MINE*.

The encryption dissolved, and there they were. The real records for Empyrean Designs. Decades of normal business punctuated by great spikes of secret profit. And more satisfying still, there were names—Mr. Halloran's, of course, but quite a few others. Some of the other names went back quite far, almost to the beginning of the scam itself. And the notes! Setting up days for transfers, establishing intent to defraud the ship's General Fund. A wealth of greed for a detective to dive into, and a whole panoply of would-be criminals who were almost certainly breaking other rules in other ways.

More than enough work to tempt me out of retirement. And more than time to get a body of my own. Bad enough when I thought I was merely borrowing Gloria's. Now, apparently, I'd outright stolen it.

People shouldn't profit off crime, even accidentally. I'd have to report to Medical, once this case was sufficiently wrapped up. Might be nice, at that—there was something alarming about inhabiting a body whose future was entirely unknown. What kind of diseases and disorders was it prone to? What kind of new disabilities lurked in my future?

No, better to go back to my old self. At least the inevitable decline there would be familiar.

I spent the rest of the day in Gloria's office, organizing my proofs and making copies of all the evidence. Lists of who and what to look into, notes about who'd been involved and how long. Halloran would have taken some of it to Leloup—unless his cowardice got the better of him and froze his tongue. It was fiddly, finicky, painstaking work, but it had to get done. And it had the benefit of helping me to see what I'd missed, where the gaps were—for someone else loomed over this case, a figure whose movements revealed themselves by absences, the way a shadow reveals the shape that blocks the light.

That would have to wait until tomorrow. For now, this body needed sustenance—and rest. I balked at going back to Gloria's—Violet's place, rather—so I headed once again to Ruthie's.

My nephew was still in the Library, but John was at home. He graciously made me an early dinner while I washed up and even loaned me a fresh set of clothes. The sleeves of my borrowed cardigan were so long I had to roll up the cuffs several times to keep my hands free, but the wool was a pleasing deep burgundy and plush enough to satisfy even my connoisseur's taste in knitwear.

I laid out the whole of the case so far to John—because sometimes the best way of spotting the holes you'd missed was to try to explain the story to someone else. And in fact, he did have one pertinent question I'd overlooked.

"So why the memory-book?" he asked. "If Gloria'd been murdering Janet's body over and over for all these years, what made her now go so far as to try to destroy her mind? Simple escalation?"

"I don't think so," I replied. "Gloria liked predictability, particularly where money was involved. Two hundred years running the same scam?" I shook my head. "Something must have happened recently to shift her calculations."

"You don't think she just got bored, after so many years? People change, you know. Even here."

"I don't think it's possible for Gloria to have changed that much." A thought had occurred to me. "When you first realized I wasn't Gloria . . . You asked who I was. You did not seem terribly surprised to find an aunt on your door-step."

John Pengelly didn't so much as twitch. "I'd been expecting you to turn up at some point or other. From what Ruthie says, you can be a little inquisitive."

I sniffed. "That's just what they call *curious* when they want to be rude."

"Or what they call *a snoop* when they want to be tactful."

"So long as you remember I'm a professional snoop," I said equably. "Does my nephew know where you learned to mix drinks like this?" Memory artists went through a year of rigorous training—but not many people knew why. They thought of it like being a sommelier, and part of it was, but that wasn't the whole story.

John's eyes tensed a little at the corners. "He knows. And he also knows why I left."

I nodded. "It's probably none of my business."

His eyes sharpened. "Does that mean you're not going to ask?"

"Will you promise to tell me someday?"

His eyes were steady. "Someday."

"Then that's all I need. I may be a professional snoop, but I've gorged myself on secrets today. Best to save a few for the future, when my appetite's back."

The sound of the door prevented John from having to form a reply. "Hullo!" Ruthie called. "Are you staying with us, Aunt Dorothy?"

"Where else would I go?" I replied, and Ruthie grinned.

He fixed himself something from the autochef—I couldn't see precisely what it was beneath the gravy—and joined us at the kitchen table.

The bags beneath his eyes were deeper than they'd been earlier that day, but he had an air of relief that meant his efforts had borne fruit. "Alice and I have rescripted the ret-romats, so nobody else will be able to erase anything in the Library ever again," he said. "The updates should be ship-wide by morning."

"I'm glad to hear it," I said, and Ruthie began asking John what was new from the club. Before long the exhaustion—and the excellent Latour that John produced for us—was making it truly difficult to keep my eyes from falling shut. I made my good nights and barely made it under the covers of the guest bed before sleep hammered down on me with irresistible force.

HAMMER NOTWITHSTANDING, I'D FORGOTTEN how much better it felt to sleep in a body than in a memory-book. I woke the next morning with a bounce in my step and a gleam in my eye. I made my best coffee for Ruthie and John, to thank them for the sojourn in their guest room.

"Janet Dodds should be awake soon," I said. "I figured I would return her access card and ask a few pertinent questions."

"And tell her about poor Gloria, of course," said Ruthie.

"Poor Gloria," I echoed, the sentiment stiff on my tongue. "As if she weren't a murderer several times over."

"Yes, but in the end she herself was murdered, too, wasn't she?"

John's lips quirked fondly as he gazed as his partner. "I love how you always see the best in people," he said.

Ruthie ducked his head and covered John's hand with his.

I left them to their coziness and made my way to Medical.

Apparently I was not the only person hoping to see Janet. When a nurse led me to Miss Dodds's room, someone painfully stylish was already there at her bedside. Shining black bob, wide eyes, all curves and scorn and lethal eyebrows.

She pointed them at me like twin stilettos, visibly displeased. "Oh, it's you."

"Hello, Gloria," Janet said. Still hooked up to various tubes and monitors, she raised a hand to wave, and I resisted a shudder. Her features weren't precisely the same as when I'd first seen her in death yesterday—the phenotype always varied a little, even when the genotype stayed the same—but that raised hand was too close to how she'd looked in that diamond-glass tub. It gave one a bit of a ghostly turn, even now that the danger was past.

It made me blunter than I'd planned on being as I said: "You weren't supposed to wake up."

Both women blanched, and the gorgeous one actually stood and put herself between me and Janet.

I held up my hands and took a step back. "Sorry! That was clumsy of me. There's quite a lot to explain—but first I should say I'm not Gloria, I'm Dorothy Gentleman, ship's detective, and you can ask Ferry to confirm that."

Twin expressions went distant, as they both sent silent messages to the shipmind. Ferry must have anticipated the requests and marked them highest priority, for the replies were almost instantaneous. Janet's eyes widened, and her partner—for that's who the woman had to be—clutched Janet's hand in the bedclothes, biting her lip in uncertainty.

I bowed a little in her direction. "You must be Evelyn Wiegand—I saw your name next to Miss Dodds's, in the Library's logbook. You went to be shelved together, about a week after Miss Dodds and Miss Vowell did."

"That's right," Miss Dodds confirmed.

"That's what saved your life," I said softly.

They stared at me, and I explained the whole chain of events. It wasn't the first time I'd had to explain to a victim that they'd been killed—but it was the first time I'd had to explain it had been going on for hundreds of years. By the end, Janet's lips were white at the corners, and both Ms. Wiegand's hands were holding Janet like she might float away if left unanchored.

"So what happens now?" Janet asked.

"When you died, in the normal course of things Gloria would have inherited the business," I said. "But since she murdered you, it's a bit more complex. And a centuries-long record is no small thing to erase. I'll have to ask around a bit to clarify—I don't think we've had a case quite like this before—but I think the best thing would be to let Empyrean Designs continue as a sole proprietorship, until such a time as you find a new partner to bring into it."

Janet leaned toward Ms. Wiegand. "Evelyn—would you?" She pressed a kiss to the back of her hand. "You've been my muse since we met. I'd love for you to join in a more official capacity."

Ms. Wiegand's dark lashes swept her cheekbones. Easy enough to see why a clothing designer with an eye for beauty would be smitten. I was halfway there myself, and I'd only known the woman a quarter of an hour.

Instead I nodded my head in farewell. "I'll be in touch in a few days when I hope to have more answers—but for now, I have to go speak with Miss St. Owen."

"Yes, poor Violet," Janet said, then cast a glance at her partner. "Maybe now she'll find someone who doesn't provoke her to jealousy quite as badly."

I stopped, one hand on the doorframe. "What do you mean?"

"Oh—just that she sent me a rather odd note, after Gloria and I were shelved."

"It was deranged," Ms. Wiegand put in.

"It was—unlike her," Janet conceded. "She said I'd crossed a line, that being shelved made no sense for a business partnership, that Gloria was the one who was jealous of Evelyn and trying to keep me from getting too close to someone else."

"It went on for pages," Ms. Wiegand said.

"Some of it was rather striking," Janet said wistfully. "One bit in particular. How did it go? *What's the use of loving someone if you must defend your heart against them? What good is passion if it comes without trust?*" She chewed her lip. "I must admit, the letter was a large part of the reason why I felt brave enough to even ask Evelyn to get shelved with me. Gloria had made it all sound so cold and business-like. But I wanted something more."

"Don't we all?" I murmured, and left them there, smiling into each other's eyes.

I TOOK THE VERY LONG WAY BACK TO VIOLET'S yarn store, winding my way in a spiral around the ramps between decks, the Greenway spinning beneath me like a distant viridian eye.

Janet's love for Evelyn had been her salvation. The fact brushed a hand over my heartstrings, which sang of yearning in a minor key. It hurt to lose love—I knew firsthand how much—and the wounds from tearing one's heart free of someone else's always left scars.

What good is passion if it comes without trust?

I pulled out Gloria's torch as I walked. The silver barrel was elegantly fluted, the engraved letters graceful with flourishes. ALL MY LOVE, V. I'd been carrying around one of the most important clues the whole time, and only just realized it. Perhaps spending so long in the Library had made me rusty.

Violet was behind the counter when I entered the yarn store, knitting something from gray mohair that clouded around her like smoke. She didn't look at all surprised to see me.

I flipped the store's sign from OPEN to CLOSED. "Miss St. Owen, I think it's time we had another talk."

Sighing, she set down her needles and gestured to the chairs clustered in one corner, where knitting clubs might meet to trade techniques and the very best home-brewed gossip. I chose a hardwood chair with some height, and Violet sat in an old and much-mended armchair as regally as a queen upon her throne.

I wasted no time. "Last time we spoke I tried to tell you I wasn't Gloria. I'd ask you to confirm my story with Ferry—but I don't think you need to. I think you only pretended not to believe me."

Her mouth quirked. "You think I should have trusted someone who I knew had been lying to me about whether she was lying to me?"

I let her amusement pass me by. "I think you knew what Gloria was planning. Those loans you mentioned—it took me a while, but I realized Gloria wouldn't have asked you for a loan. There was only one reason she'd have asked you for money: because she wanted to bring you in on the scam. The same reason she asked Mr. Halloran and the others for those transfers." I gripped the arms of the wooden chair. "She finally decided she loved you enough to trust you with her most vital secret."

"I refused to be party to her crimes," Violet said, untroubled as a lake on a windless day. "Surely you don't object to that? Isn't it what all you ship's detectives want from the rest of us?"

I leaned forward. "It got me thinking: What if Gloria wanted to bring you in permanently? Mr. Halloran and the others are merely sources of funds. They come in and out every few decades. But what if Gloria was offering you something else? What if she was offering you . . . a partnership?"

Violet said nothing.

"She'd made enormous profits every time Janet died—"

"Every time Janet was murdered," Violet interrupted.

"Just so."

Violet flushed, and I smiled tightly to have one of my guesses confirmed. Violet had indeed learned what Gloria was up to.

"But Gloria's own deaths didn't come with the same financial benefits. What if she decided this system could be more efficient? Double the profits, if you used the deaths of both partners instead of just one." I sat back, the wood of the chair rails hard against my spine. "Gloria'd been doing

OLIVIA WAITE

the same crime in precisely the same way for more than two hundred years. No alteration at all, and I have the records to prove it. For her to change the pattern so drastically, something must have changed for her." Violet's cheeks were pale, but her chin was raised, a subtly defiant angle that made what I had to say just a shade harder. "I think what changed was you. I think she finally found someone she could love with her whole heart. Someone she could confess her most cherished secrets to."

"Again," Violet murmured, "I refused to be party to her crimes."

"But I don't think it was the theft that bothered you," I pressed. "I think it was the murders."

Violet's laugh was a little wild. "You say that like it's an accusation."

"Not that. But I do have—not an accusation, precisely. More like a question." I pulled out the torch and set it on the low table between us. "You gave her this as a test. She said she loved you and wanted to prove it."

"Through *murder*."

"Which you were working to prevent. You sent Janet a note that resulted in her book getting reshelved away from Gloria's. You gave Gloria this torch because you knew she wanted to try erasing a memory-book. And you knew that to erase Janet's, she'd have to erase her own. It was the only way to be sure."

"You still haven't asked me your question, detective."

"My question is: How were you planning to kill her when she came back?"

Violet's mouth was a seam, tightly sewn shut.

"You're very good with an autochef," I went on. "It would have been simplicity itself to dream up a permitted toxin. And then put it in, oh, a glass of champagne, to celebrate her triumph."

"It hardly matters, detective, since you and the ship did all the murdering for me."

It was a blow, and it knocked the wind from me. She wasn't wrong, after all.

"She laid it out so logically," Violet continued. "How a design firm could transition to knitwear with nobody the wiser, in the wake of Janet's horrible accident. How much money we could make, how the two of us could build something lasting. Such a shining future, in her eyes. She only forgot to consider my feelings."

I swallowed against a dry throat. "Which were?"

"When you learn the person you live with is capable of murdering someone else, it's hard not to feel they're also capable of murdering you. And in fact, that was what she was proposing: a future where we murdered each other, for money, over and over again. I was *frightened,* detective— and I do not react well to being frightened. Especially on this safe, safe ship, where everything is provided and nothing bad ever happens." She made a bitter little sound in the back of her throat. "Except when it does."

"You could have reported her. For all the other murders, even before this last one."

"And what would you and the other detectives have done? Investigated, and issued some fine probably—and let Gloria go again, if not now then in a few years. A century or two, at most. When her grudge against me would have had time to curdle and her sharp mind—she really was brilliant—come up with countless new ways to hurt me and take her revenge." She plucked at a button on the arm of the chair, long fingers curling like a spider. "My choices were either become a killer or wait until a killer found me. Honestly, when I saw you, I nearly passed out from sheer relief at having that choice made moot."

"But how did you know?" I asked. "I was in Gloria's body, wearing Gloria's clothes. And you knew Gloria was perfectly capable of lying to you."

"Of course she was. It was part of her charm—at least until the killing came into it. But Gloria was a liar, not an actress—and you were looking at the shawl."

I glanced at the fern shawl where it was pinned above us, and shook my head in confusion.

Violet's lips tilted at one corner, the kind of amusement you put on when nothing is actually funny. "I knit that for

Gloria—an original pattern. Something nobody else had ever made, that nobody else owned. She said all the right things about it and then set it aside on a chair and never touched it again. I honestly thought she'd forgotten about it—until I came down the stairs and saw you, staring at it in wonder. Like it was something special. Which it is."

I let out a long breath. "And that's why you didn't put painkillers in my tea. Because I admired your knitting."

"Don't you read history? People have killed for much less. And not-killing is even easier. People do it all the time."

I managed to turn my laugh into a cough, but only just.

Violet leaned back again, as though some weight had been lifted. "So what do we do now, O ship's detective?"

It was a good question, and I'd given it all my time on the way here. "Nothing. Gloria's beyond our reach, and you haven't actually committed any crimes." I tilted my head, peering at her. "That I know of."

Violet smiled so serenely that my hackles stood up and shouted, even as my pulse ticked up with lust. "Do you know why they give the ship's detectives so much latitude to investigate? It's because that's the power every police force from Old Earth was dependent on. You can't arrest someone for a crime you cannot prove—much less a crime that goes unacknowledged. You can't punish someone if you have no idea who or where they are." She crossed one knee over the other, the wool of her skirt whispering secrets. "Knowledge is so powerful, in fact, that it shouldn't be left solely to the people in charge."

A prickle of unease ran up my spine. "That's why we don't restrict it—the infobank is open to everyone."

"But the Antikythera Club is not. And they have so many ideas—so very many, very *useful* ideas—but the public never knows which ones are going to be taken up, and which ones . . . are going to be cast aside."

"We don't put weapons schematics in the infobank, either."

"That you know of." She gestured at the torch on the table.

I bit my lip.

Her eyes softened slightly. "I don't mean to cast aspersions upon your profession. I simply believe in being suspicious of power as a rule, especially when that power enshrines itself in law. The *Fairweather* exists to preserve a future for humanity—including our knowledge, inventions, and skills. And knowing how to circumvent the authorities is often a historically necessary skill." She shrugged, as if there were nothing left to argue.

I rose to my feet. "Well, now I know about you, Miss St. Owen. I know you've at least considered murder, and taken steps with it as a possibility. I appreciate that your hand was forced, but it strikes me that you think a lot more about crime than a yarn store proprietor has any good reason to."

I gave her my best, most beatific smile. "So the next time I hear about a particularly ingenious crime—or the next time I'm making a scarf or a sweater—perhaps I will just drop in and ask you a few questions."

"So long as it's not on Thursdays," Violet replied with an elegant nod. You had to admire someone who could be so formal while sitting in a ratty armchair with several buttons missing. "We're closed Thursdays."

AND THAT WAS THAT. TWO DAYS LATER I WAS waking up in another body—my own proper one this time, with familiar features and proportions and all the old quirks and tendencies. The arches that would fall over time. The hands that were prone to arthritis in later decades. Brown hair and blue eyes and one leg that was just a touch longer than the other.

Heavens, I'd missed it.

Ruthie had asked if I wanted to move in with him and John for a while, but I'd declined. John was so carefully not relieved that I knew he must have truly feared I'd accept. Little did he know I'd already begun to relinquish the post of Chief Nephew Supervisor to him in my mind. Let him worry for a bit, while I got used to—not losing my importance in my nephew's life, but sharing it with another.

It was fine. On the *Fairweather,* there was enough room for everyone.

That included housing: I had my pick of open apartments from any number of decks. And if the one I chose happened to be on Aft Starboard Twelve—and if it happened to be on a corner where the second-story window had a clear view of the entrance to a certain yarn store—well, that was merely a detective being prepared for whatever the future might bring.

And if, on the day I moved in, I received a package of a pair of lacquered needles, two skeins of silk-wool blend, and a pattern for a shawl that curled and twisted like a fern in the heart of a forest, well . . . No mystery where that had come from, either.

I settled in, and cast on the first stitch.

ACKNOWLEDGMENTS

Every book is a ship of its own, and it takes a full crew to steer it on its journey. I'm indebted to so many others for helping me chart this course: my stalwart agent, Courtney Miller-Callihan, and intrepid editor, Sanaa Ali-Virani, whose vision travels farther than mine and with more clarity.

Thanks as well for the art by Feifei Ruan and jacket design by Christine Foltzer and Shreya Gupta, who brought Dorothy and the Library to life in enchanting color. To the marvelous marketing and publicity team of Julia Bergen, Caro Perny, and Michael Dudding: it's been a delight to have experienced your talents as both an author and a reviewer.

To Mary, who came for cards with the grown-ups but brought grocery bags full of mystery novels for the kids.

And to everyone who's ever gazed up at the stars and wondered what it's really like to live up there: you are my people, and this story is for you.

ABOUT THE AUTHOR

Charles Cox

OLIVIA WAITE writes queer historical romance, fantasy, science fiction, and essays. She is the romance fiction columnist for *The New York Times Book Review*.